Six Short Stories

By

Mark Hayes Peacock

The Thoughts Of Two Writers About These Stories

"Mark Hayes Peacock is a very careful and deliberate author, always sensitive to inspiring

his readers to proceed from paragraph to paragraph. His characters

are people we come to know and his plots capture our attention to

pursue what will happen next. Their resolution makes for a very

rewarding and satisfying experience. His focus and insights have

resulted in stories that stick in your mind and inspire you to turn the

page to open the next story."

LaMoine MacLaughlin

Award winner, Jade Ring Prize for fiction

First Poet Laureate, Amery, Wisconsin

Executive Director, The Northern Lakes School for

the Arts

*

"Looking for quick reads that are everything from gently thought provoking, heart warming, clever, humorous and even a little twisted at times? This collection might be just what you are looking for. Set in different times and places, each story has its own movie set that comes alive effortlessly in my mind."

Judy Breuer

Former columnist, The Budgeteer, Duluth, Minnesota

Health Educator/Advocate and Podcaster

We Gotta Help Bomber!

by

Mark Hayes Peacock

No one ever said Bomber was stupid. He just was trapped, trapped in the way so many guys in small towns get trapped: there's always a vacant bar stool or space at the café counter with someone waiting to hear, perhaps once again, the story of how Bomber caught the 45 yard pass and bombed down the sidelines, shedding tackles all the way, to score the victory over our super-rival, Palmerton High. Bombing through to victory is how Bomber got his nickname.

Bomber, whose proper name is Bernard, willingly obliged his listeners. Trapped in town by his reputation, our local hero had taken odd jobs over the years, working sometimes for the Village, sometimes as a field hand on call, sometimes at the lumberyard until a national chain put it out of business, and sometimes just as a handyman for elderly widows that needed some help. Bomber was a guy with a big heart. But the result of all that part-time work and piecemeal jobs was a slim retirement income, mostly from Social Security.

After his retirement, Bomber would join us for coffee fairly regularly, "us" being me, away from my accounting office on a welcome break; Jack, whose clothing store was under siege by stores in the large mall in Palmerton seven miles to our west; Billy, our town barber; Stanley, our jeweler, who has been trying to sell his store for several years now; and Barton, our retired feed mill manager who'd become president of our Village board.

Billy the barber, Barton and I were the exceptions: the others felt pressured by big outside interests and helpless to fight back.

We always knew when Bomber would be joining us because his silver, steadily-turning brown pickup truck would be parked smack in front of the café door. The poor battered thing seemed to sag in the middle and even the plow Bomber stuck on its front end in Winter failed to give the truck any semblance of dignity.

"Just as I figured they would," said Bomber one day recently. "They've gone and raised our rents by $300 a month. I don't know what I'm going to do."

"We could see that coming from a mile away," said Jack, whose clothing store was under pressure from his suppliers and competitors. "The minute those big outfits come in, everything changes. They've already bought several apartment complexes in Palmerton and it was just a matter of time until they came over here."

"So what are you going to do?" Billy asked Bomber.

"Damned if I know," said Bomber. "I don't know where I can go. I can't afford a house and apartments are out of my range now, too—if I could even find another apartment. There aren't any."

"Maybe you could come up with a girlfriend that needs a roommate?" ventured Stanley.

"At my age? I've got enough trouble. No thanks!"

"Stan, you just want to sell him a ring for her—whoever she might be!" said Billy.

We laughed.

Shirley, our waitress, set another pot of coffee on the table for us. She rolled her eyes as Big John's voice bellowed from his table in the back. Big John was notorious for his opposition to taxes. We all figured it was a matter of time until some sort of SWAT Team came down John's driveway to haul him off to court. "What you really need to do is to take your rifle down to the Capitol and just start shooting!" he bellowed to the young man at his table. "Show 'em that you mean it!"

"Say that to the wrong person and you've got some real trouble," said Barton in a lowered voice as he leaned in to us.

But we were used to Big John and his rants. He was a member of the Posse Comitatus group over in Poskin and always was willing to rant about government overreach and how we need to resist the IRS. He had a grudge: he lost his farm some years back when he refused to pay taxes. I remember the sign at the end of his driveway: "No Trespassing. IRS Agents Will Be Shot." He was loud and usually had a listener or two to hang on his rants about governmental overreach.

Today, however, we tuned out Big John; our attention focused on Bomber's predicament: no place to go, no money, and limited options.

Barton looked around our table. "Well," he said, "I'm sure we all can figure out something." But it was obvious from our faces that none of us had a clue about how to give Bomber the help he needed.

"I'm buying for everybody this morning," offered Billy, who sagely spared Bomber the embarrassment of being short the money for his coffee.

It was at coffee the next day that Jack brought his bad news: his supplier of jeans had cut him off. "I don't have the sales volume they want these days," said Jack. "That's the end."

"That's crazy," I said. "You buy their stuff; you pay shipping; you sell their stuff and send them the money. What does it cost them to have you as a simple line item on their computer?"

"It doesn't make sense to me, either," said Jack. "But I think that's it for us. Without items like jeans and overalls, there's no business to sell. We might be able to sell the building, but to whom? And for what? If I can get a buyer, I'll be sending you guys post cards from Arizona."

For some reason, all our heads turned slowly to Stanley.

"What?"

"Business," I said. "How's business?"

"Diamonds are forever, as they say," said Stanley. "And if they sit in my display cases forever, there's no money coming in. People go now to the big outfits, places like The Jewel Box over in Palmerton or even shops in The City. It's been slow, too slow."

"You remember I told you guys about my conversation with Timmons?" said Jack. Tyler "Toby" Timmons is our Congressman and we can't say that, as a group, we're fond of him. "When I explained our dilemma to him, his response was to tell me what he said he told farmers in our area: 'Get big or get out!' So there was no help and not much sympathy. If we're going to survive, we're going to have to do it by ourselves."

"Can't say we're doing great at that," said Billy.

"You know," said Barton, " there was a time—back when I was a kid here—that we had three gas stations in town and two grocery stores, a hardware store (you know, the old blacksmith shop, that was part of it) and several clothing stores, including the store your grandparents had, Jack."

Jack nodded. "I folded sweaters there when I was a kid."

"And that's the business you bought, right?" I said.

"Yes."

Billy was looking around. "So, where's Bomber?" he asked.

We shrugged. No one knew.

"Maybe he found that girlfriend?" said Stanley.

"Still pushing the idea of a ring Stan?" said Billy. We laughed and it felt good to laugh in the face of the latest dismal news.

"So" said Barton solemnly. "How are we going to help Bomber?"

He looked around at a group of blank faces. None of us had the foggiest idea of how to help our friend and town hero.

Big John was in his corner ranting about governmental overreach. Shirley approached us with our second round of coffee and a tray of fresh donuts.

"Any of your girl friends need a roommate?" asked Stanley. "We know of a possibility."

"Bomber?" she said.

Stanley smiled. "You're quick," he said.

""He's been with every single girl in town," said Shirley. "There's no one left."

"No one but maybe you,' grinned Stanley.

"Sorry, son; Harold and I still are going strong. Thirty five years. And just for that, you'd better leave me a big fat tip this morning, smarty pants!"

Shirley always gave as good as she got. We love her.

"Well, maybe sleeping on it can come up with some ideas," said Barton. We nodded but each of us knew there wasn't much to be optimistic about when it came to helping out little guys up against big obstacles.

The pressure had been building on our town for several years now. Palmerton was not that far away and the chain grocery store there even sold milk for less than our store could. Even our gasoline was priced higher, reflecting the small distance further from the refinery's jobber. People who had jobs over in Palmerton shopped there on their way home from work. It was almost like Palmerton glittered out there on the horizon while our town was bathed in shadows.

Maybe that led to a sense that somehow we had an inferiority complex. I've always been convinced that our people have no idea about how good they really are. But our low average income, especially for those people who worked in town, rather than in Palmerton, raised a strong argument against what I think.

Bomber wasn't around for coffee the next morning either, so we felt free to try to figure out how to help him.

"If we could find someone who'd rent him a room, perhaps we could chip in to help pay the rent," offered Barton. "The problem is, I just can't think of anyone."

"Bomber has too much pride," said Billy. "It would have to be done on the sly. Whoever did it would have to quote him a phony rent figure."

"He knows how much rents are going for," I said. "He'd figure something was up."

We sat in glum silence.

"Maybe we need to put something in your coffee," said Shirley, as she set a fresh pot on the table. "You guys look pretty down."

"Yeah, we're thinking," said Jack.

"That's dangerous! she said. "Bomber?"

"Of course."

"It's sure no fun being a broke local hero," she said. "I always told him he sold himself too cheap."

"Didn't he help your Dad with hay bailing a few years back?" asked Barton.

Shirley nodded. "That he did!" Then, deciding to pour for us, she added: "And he worked hard, too. Dad said he could hardly keep up. The man was an ox, he said." When she finished her pouring, she looked around the restaurant. "So, where is he?"

"Dunno," said Stanley. "We haven't seen him for a few days."

"I was at the bar last night and he wasn't there," said Billy.

Deciding to shift the conversation, Jack said, "I've got someone coming to look at the building on Friday. We'll see what happens."

"Will they continue the clothing store?" I asked.

"I don't know. But I doubt it. Right now, and no offense to you guys, I just want to sell the place and try to retire. Myrtle really wants us to head out to Arizona."

"Why there?" asked Stanley. " Rattlesnakes and tumbleweeds. It's too hot and the coffee there is lousy!"

"So, how do you know that?" asked Barton.

"My sister told me. She's in Florida and says I could sell plenty of jewelry down there, what with all those wealthy New Yorkers and rich widows."

"We could send Bomber down there," offered Stanley. "Have some rich widow take him in."

"Still trying to get Bomber that ring, eh?" laughed Billy.

"Hey, it's not that bad of an idea," responded Stanley.

I thought he might be serious.

When we met on Monday the following week, Bomber was absent again, Jack's real estate hopes had been dashed, and Stanley hadn't had a sale in several days. "Not even some earrings" he moaned.

"My watch needs a battery," I said. Stanley nodded. Sixteen bucks for a watch battery didn't buy much in the way of groceries.

"You heard the latest?" said Barton. "There's an outfit coming to talk with the township about building a hog processing factory just out of town. I'm told the company is one of many owned by a Chinese conglomerate."

"I heard about it yesterday," said Billy. "Some of the guys that came in had heard about it and didn't like the idea."

"It's jobs," said Barton. "We can use the jobs."

"So, how many?" said Jack. "Feeding slop to pigs probably can't pay much, either. There are jobs and then there are jobs. Hell, look at Bomber. Isn't he our prime example of the payoff of those kinds of jobs?"

"Where is he, anyway," asked Barton. "Anyone seen him lately?" All heads shook negative.

"Congressman Timmons is backing the hog project," said Billy "Says we need to meet the market. China loves pork so we can give them plenty of pork."

"Yeah, but the stench," said Jack. "That, and the pee and shit. Where does that go?"

"That's right," said Stanley. "I live down in that area, if that's where they're talking about. How am I going to sell my house if the air smells to high heaven? And how about the water and pollution? And I'm not the only one who lives down in that area. There are a number of homes. Billy, are you sure about this?"

Billy nodded. "All I know is what the guys in the shop were talking about, but they sure seemed to know. Timmons was even down there on the property, walking the acreage with the people that came into town to check it out."

"Damn!" I said. "We elect the guy to represent us and all he does is work against us, it seems. Why can't we turn him out?"

"Gerrymandering," said Barton. "He never has real opposition. This is as safe a district as any in the State, so he's been in Congress for a long time."

"Yeah, and it looks like he'll stay there, too," said Jack. "You remember what he told me, that we had to get bigger or get out? Well, a hog factory makes raising pigs into something really big."

"And then we need to get out," said Stanley. "That would be great if we could."

I had an appointment so I got up from the table, laid some bills for Shirley on the table, and paid our bill up at the register. I guessed that we would hear something official soon about that pig factory.

But it wasn't pig factory news that energized us at coffee the next day, those few of us who made it in.

The snow began just after sundown. It was an avalanche of snow, or so it seemed, with huge flakes coming down hard and constantly all night long with no letup. Snowdrifts were as tall as I am, so no traffic was moving at all. And it kept on coming. The café was open, though, and Shirley, faithful as ever, had coffee ready for the few of us. Steaming hot black coffee, the perfect antidote for impossible white snow. We couldn't see clearly through the iced-up windows, but we could hear the backup beeping and the scraping and see the flashing yellow and red lights as our crews struggled to open a path for the hardy few who'd dare to venture out.

"Stanley called me," said Billy. "He said he isn't going anywhere until the roads get cleared. Said he'd see us tomorrow if things got better."

"Yeah, out where he lives is around the last to get plowed," I said.

Shirley pointed to the TV above the counter. Governor Warren had declared an emergency and asked for Federal help, so I guess this storm was bad all over. Congressman Timmons was being interviewed. "Federal emergency money is our money," he said. "Our taxes are too high! This country was built on the blood, sweat and tears of individuals. We should be able to take care of ourselves. We don't need more big government! I think we all should object to the Governor's move to ask for Federal help."

"Good old Timmons," said Barton with a shake of his head. "Always ready to help the plain old little folks."

Shirley stopped by our table, coffee pot in hand. "I just talked to my mother," she said. "Bomber was out plowing every driveway in her neighborhood. He plowed hers and she went out to offer him some money. He said no and kept on plowing driveways up and down her street non-stop. He moved all the snow into the middle of the road so the crews could come with a loader and dump truck to haul it out to the dump area."

"And that," said Barton, "is why our friend Bomber has no retirement money. Too damned generous. Generous to a fault. What do we do about a guy like him?"

It took more than three days for our crews to clear the streets and get things operational again. Some people had lost power; heavy snow had broken tree branches that fell across power lines. Telephones had been out of commission, too.

We still hadn't seen Bomber.

He was the only one of us "regulars" absent from coffee the next morning. Billy came in at a near-run and slid into the booth opposite me.

"Turn on the TV!" he shouted.

Shirley moved to the end of the counter and turned on the television.

"What's going on?" I asked.

"Toby Timmons got shot last night," said Billy.

To say that we were stunned is an understatement. All coffee cups suddenly were put down on our table. Shirley scanned several stations. No news, just network morning programming. The TV was silent on a Timmons' shooting. Then, "breaking news"; coverage of

Toby Timmons' shooting began. *A suspect surrendered peacefully and was taken into custody immediately. No motive for the shooting can be reported at this time. Representative Timmons was shot at close range while holding a Q and A at the Palmerton Legion Hall.*

We watched. We saw the live footage as the handcuffed suspect was led from jail.

"God, that guy looks like Bomber!" said Jack.

"Hell, it IS Bomber!" said Billy.

"It's like he listened to Big John?" I said.

The television was reporting now that Toby Timmons did not survive the shooting.

"Just as well," said Jack. "Good riddance to him!"

"I think, though," mused Barton, "Bomber just solved all his problems."

"What?" I said, incredulous. 'That's nuts!"

"Not so fast! Think it through," said Barton sagely. "Bomber needs a place to live, right? He needs to eat, right? He's not a young guy and he's probably going to need some health care in the near future. You've seen how he's been hobbling a bit lately? So now Bomber is set up for the rest of his life. Whether he pleads guilty or pleads not guilty, whether he's in jail or in prison, for the rest of his life he has a roof over his head, he has heat, and enough to eat. And it costs him nothing, at least financially. That's why I said he's solved his problems."

No one said a word. The rest of us sat silently, absorbing the logic.

As I told you, no one ever said Bomber was stupid.

I Loved That Bike!

by

Mark Hayes Peacock

Damn, I sure loved that bike! I'd had it in my heart for years and at last I could afford it. Sue and I would go cruising, even in the rain and when the wind was not nice, but the twisty country roads and hillsides paved with multi-colored leaves in the Fall brought more joy to us than just about anything else could.

And the bike was easier to keep pristine than my cars ever were. I'd polish the black paint until Sue could put on lipstick in its reflection and we could see our tattoos, to say nothing of the way I'd shine the chrome until it popped your eyeballs.

Yes, I loved that bike! There wasn't much left of it though or of me either after I hit that tree.

It was a day when Sue wasn't along. She'd gone to visit her mother, that old bat. She's never liked me, says I'm a bad influence on Sue, but how long has it been now, more than twenty years? Long ago she quit trying to get me to marry Sue; marriage for us just didn't seem to fit. My older sister Ginny, who knows everything because she's a psychologist and has a Ph.D. and makes sure I'm reminded of those things, told me I owed it to Sue to marry her. "After all," said Ginny, "she raised your two kids and because of the law if something happens to you, your kids get the house and she gets nothing. Some man you are to treat her that way!"

Ginny had the accident figured out, too. "You claim you blacked out before going off the road; but you really didn't. You tried to check out."

Just about every bone I have was broken and I was hurting too much to give her an argument.

"Take a look at your life," she continued. "Here you are, middle aged and still at work just running wood through a saw, never a promotion, never reaching your potential. Your kids relate to you only to ask for money. Your vacations have been just about any possible cruise a person can take—you've been there, done that—

and weekends are one drunk after another so all you have to look forward to is another hangover. So you ask, subconsciously of course, 'is this all there is?' The answer is, there's just more of the same coming; why continue? Life's not worth it!

"And there is Sue. You're stuck with an overly dependent needy person who's stood by you for years because she's afraid she can't function without you. Maybe she's right. It's too tough for you to face the truth and tell everyone 'I quit', so you just 'black out' and smack into a large black walnut tree.

"The only trouble is, just like the rest of your life, you screwed it up. Just like Dad and Mom used to tell you, focus, quit messing around and finish what you started!"

I managed to croak "Please leave" and she did leave just as the nurse came with another pain pill.

Ginny's a jerk but I think that she does love me. I just wish she liked me. I know she didn't like my bike.

Sue came in just after I got my pill. She came every day in the early afternoon. "Why don't you just let me die?" I asked her. She shook her head.

That was before the seventeen surgeries. I still hurt and I couldn't walk, hobbled maybe with crutches or a walker and someone nearby. That person usually was Sue, never my children but sometimes Ginny. I think Ginny came to make sure she had it figured right. I was some kind of a case, maybe better than she would get in her psychology practice. So I was her experiment and maybe even written up for an article she'd submit to some professional magazine of hers.

Ginny came at me again after that first go-round, aiming this time at my so-called "rebelliousness". "You just wanted to pimp Mom and Dad," she said, "so you didn't study and decided no one was going to tell you what to do and how to talk, so there you were, saying 'ain't' all the time and you knew it drove Mom up the wall and you dared them to ground you by coming in at all hours of the morning and out all night. The thing is, you're smart, real smart, but you decided to go screw it up, why I don't know. You'll always be just a *little* brother!"

When I asked her to leave this time she departed quickly.

"So why don't you let me die?" I'd ask and Sue would shake her head and bring me home again to our shabby little house on the edge of the industrial park where I used to work and she would feed me and put up with my moaning and my anger and help me in and out of bed and my big chair—and why? I never did figure her out.

Sue and I met at the big bar in town, the one with the live band on Friday nights, the one with the loud wet t-shirt nights and the hooting and hollering, the one in the news when the drunk girl walked home after two a.m. and got hit by the semi because she was walking in the middle of the road. Sue, I saw her dancing by herself, moving easily to the music, making the chrome studs on the rear of her jeans undulate back and forth and I had to go dance with her. She welcomed that with a smile. And then we got to talking and I bought her a few drinks and then I drove her home in my muddy red truck, the one with the wide-stance tires and fender flares, and I got her phone number and after that we got to know each other in the best of ways. But I never did figure her out.

After she moved in with me she knew I'd always wanted a bike like the one I eventually got. She even bought herself a helmet before I had the bike; that was the way she was with me. But after the accident, after the blacking out, life would have been easier for her if she'd let me die. I'll never figure why she didn't.

All that, of course, was before the stroke, before I couldn't ask her that question anymore. All I can do now is roll my eyes. The tube restricts my head so I can't even roll it from side to side. If I can manage a moan the nurses know I need another pain pill, but it's a shot instead because I can't swallow pills anymore. I still feel the needles going in.

My kids? They haven't been here for weeks or maybe longer. Ginny's come and doesn't lecture me anymore or analyze me. I'm not sure why that is. Sue comes every day, just like she did when I was a mess of broken bones and bleeding organs. Sometimes Ginny comes when Sue is here. They talk together and sometimes talk about me as if I can't hear what they are saying. Ginny is like my Mom and Dad, pretty practical, so she wants to make sure Sue has things arranged for when I die.

I suppose if there were some way to signal it I'd consent to marrying Sue now. Hospice has a chaplain who comes from time to time—I'm not sure how often; days slide into days and the room is kept dark so I'm never sure of what time it might be—and judging by her voice, a young voice that has shape and gentleness, I'm guessing the chaplain probably is a good looking young woman. I'm sure she could do a wedding if a wedding could be done. But how legal will it be for a man to marry when he can't do more than blink? "Do you take this woman? Blink if you assent." Now, wouldn't that be a rich event! I can just see it: all the nurses in the place gathered around to make sure that this marriage GOT DONE! Whoopee! It might even make the papers.

My parents always said I had a great imagination.

Well, I did imagine, I imagined for years how it would be to ride that bike, to feel the wind through my hair—no helmet for me!—and the banking of the machine as I took it around a tight curve and then goosed the accelerator and heard the blast of the exhaust and felt the G's as the front wheel lifted off the pavement. I imagined for years what it would be like to sit at the stop light and hear the "potato, potato" of the idling engine under my seat and then lift my feet and hurtle away from the traffic as the light turned green. I imagined what it would be like to ride in tandem with another bike beside mine and how we'd weave in and out of traffic but still end up riding side by side, two headlights stabbing into the dark as night came, and the urgent sound of that chrome-finned engine throbbing under my seat.

My imagination turned out to be reality but with Sue on the back, her arms around my waist, the chrome brace behind her back so she could lean away when she got tired of holding onto me.

But just a bit ago Sue got tired of holding onto me. She and Ginny were talking again, as if I couldn't hear. "There must be some way of letting him go," said Sue. "No!" Ginny responded. "No, he's my brother."

I was astonished.

"But keeping him like this cruel."

"Miracles happen," said Ginny. "We don't pull the plug."

They talked about it with the chaplain when she came in. I said I thought that, judging from her voice, the chaplain is a pretty young thing but she turns out to be a capable woman, a woman who knows her stuff. "That's not so easy," she said. "Let me refresh myself here." Trying to size up the situation, she turned to Sue. "You are his companion, not his wife?" she asked.

"Yes."

"And you are his sister?"

"His older sister, yes."

The chaplain sat silently for a while. Then she said: "Neither of you have legal standing to make a decision about his future. Neither of you can order life support to be removed, at least under the current circumstances. There is such a thing as conservatorship, that's for finances, and there's guardianship, which deals with health care decisions. Because he can't name anyone for those functions, the court can appoint an 'outsider' to make those kinds of decisions. But becoming one is very costly and it's a lengthy process—even longer if someone objects."

I'm pretty sure at that point the chaplain looked at the two of them and frowned, maybe even shook her head.

"I'm his sister," said Ginny. "We don't pull the plug!"

"But this is awful!" said Sue. "He'd hate being like this."

"I'm not so sure of that!" snapped Ginny.

The chaplain left after giving Sue and Ginny her card.

They say that the hearing is the last thing to go. Ain't true! I hear every bit of what's said. Hearing's not the last thing to go; I am.

And so here we are, or should I say here I am, brain dead they say but I still can hear and I might even be thinking—who would ever know, least of all me—and I have two women fighting

over me and they both love me in some way or other.

I guess I love them, too.

But, damn, I sure loved that bike!

True Justice

by

Mark Hayes Peacock

An eagle wafted on the updraft, swooping in a wide circle, scoping the lake below for his morning meal. The wind was out of the east, which is usually not good for fishing, and that explained the lone person in the aluminum boat far below. No one else was on the water this morning. Wise fishermen were enjoying a late cup of coffee instead of trying their luck and finding out that the eagle above shared their same fortune: empty-handed and empty talons. To its south half-a-mile a pair of eagles tumbled, locked talon to talon with Spring urgency, but right now on our eagle's agenda food was first. A drift to the east promised chipmunks and perhaps a mouse, so a slight wing dip moved him in that direction. He heard a quiet crack and saw a human's gyrations on a large machine moving along the green grass below. Sometimes machines like that flushed food the eagle liked. Another circle and the eagle might spot anything tempting that emerged. But then the machine stopped and no food appeared.

Catch and release often meant a dead fish floating on the water, and so the eagle circled around again and watched as the human in the aluminum boat dropped its catch slowly and deliberately into the water. It was an odd looking fish, long and skinny, and it didn't float or wriggle but sank quickly, as did a small rectangular thing the fisherman dangled into the water and then let go. The eagle saw the boat begin to move to the south, quickly; there was no trolling or line casting; the human obviously was finished for the day. Chipmunks and mice seemed more promising, so the eagle shifted his attention again to spotting prey that might assuage his hunger.

*   *   *

The thing that sticks in my mind from one of those ultimately boring interdenominational meetings is what the Baptist attorney said to me during a break. "If you're looking for true justice in this life, you're bound to be disappointed," he confided. Somehow, I've never forgotten that counsel. Maybe that's why I gave close attention to the couple I'd married a few years before.

There had been a shooting, a murder, and both Charlene and Derek seemed to be implicated, or, at least, both had motives for doing in Randall Dodge. And as a priest, I have an interest in honesty, truth and justice. Maybe it's just that I've seen too many television movies about priests who somehow manage to solve mysteries, which, on the surface, seems to be way out of character. But we have many different personalities in my calling and I need to be true to mine. I just don't want people who turn out to be innocent to be put through the trials of an investigation. I do like to see justice served.

Because I was concerned about the couple, I invited Charlene to visit with me first. During our pre-wedding counseling sessions, she seemed the perfect match for Derek. She was beautiful, spunky and competitive, smart and charming, a good catch. She was a trophy wife; a tall, slim blonde, my grandfather would have called her "a classy dame". I'd shot next to them at the rifle range, where Derek had taught her during their courtship. She got to be pretty good very quickly, not as good as he, for he's a professional, and she enjoyed going fishing with the two of us. Shooting against them, a friendly competition, did help me to improve and it did earn me a small share of trophies, nothing to write home about but I did well for myself. After I got used to having her along when we fished, I let her run my ancient aluminum boat with its old but reliable 35 h.p. Johnson tiller steering. Derek, who had a newer aluminum boat of the same length as mine but with a steering wheel, had no problem turning over the helm to her. As I said, Charlene was very capable. We all had fun together. But since they don't shoot together or fish together anymore, I don't either. It's more fun when there's competition, so my guns and poles have been sitting mostly idle.

I offered her a cup of my instant coffee, which she declined. She sat, primly poised in the same chair she'd sat in during our counseling before her marriage., her tanned feet showcased by narrow strap sandals, sunglasses perched atop her head, definitely an "outdoorsy" girl. I have a comfortable office: the prettiest stained glass windows in the church grace my space and in that morning's sunlight shafts of ruby red slanted across the two leather chairs flanking my well polished wooden table. I keep it clear for meetings like this.

"After our wedding things turned out to be different than I thought they would be," she said. "I figured we were compatible in just about all respects, but, oh, how wrong I was!"

"How so?"

"I tried, I really did. We'd go shooting together. He taught me, said I was a 'natural'. Well, I did get to be pretty good and picked up a couple of trophies. I mean, I'm not like he is; he's a professional. And that meant that he spent hours down at the range, practicing. If it wasn't that, it was fishing and sometimes golf. I hate golf! So after that early togetherness, things began to evaporate.

"The hard part of all this is that Derek really has no ambition, no urging to try to better himself. He goes to work, comes home, and shuts the door of his mind until it's time to go to work the next day. Or he comes home from work and heads down to the rifle range. I used to go with him, but then I got the feeling that my being part of that didn't really matter anymore. And I don't think counseling helped either of us. Counseling didn't keep us together."

I took the risk: "I understand they've talked with you about the Randall Dodge case?"

"So, he told you? Well, yes."

"And?"

"There is no 'and'. I told them what I know. Someone shot Randy while he was mowing the yard. I was grocery shopping. I have the grocery slip with the date and time to prove it."

"They think you have a motive?"

"Yes, they do."

I said nothing while she sat.

Finally, she said, "Look, everyone knows Randy was a cheat. I knew that going in. I figured, if that's his hobby, he can have at it! But that's not enough to go shoot him; I'm used to his ways; I lived with them. I've had it pretty good, you know; why would I jeopardize a good thing? Besides, I don't own a gun. I always used one of Derek's. He liked to let me use the one he learned on, the Winchester from his grandfather."

"I can't imagine being comfortable with 'his ways'," I said.

"That's because you're a priest. You've never been in a marriage situation—or part of a couple, for that matter. Right?"

"There was life before ordination."

She smiled, tilted her head in a small but saucy cock and gave me a long sizing up.

"So what do you recommend?

"I'm not sure."

"Well, don't recommend reconciliation. I'm not going back to Derek. Not after this. Definitely, never to him."

"There's a will?"

"Of course. I'm well taken care of. And Randy has no one in a position to challenge it."

"How about his business interests? Were you involved in them?"

"No. He did all his own work, all the deciding, all the financing, all the contracting; he did it all. And he did it well. But that's all in the hands of the lawyers at this point. Maybe his subcontractors will buy the business or some of it."

With that, she shifted her purse onto her lap and got up. As she thanked me for my time and for caring, she extended her hand.

I took it and then watched through the door window as she got into the cream colored Bentley, dropped her sunglasses from her hair to her eyes, rolled back the sunroof, and drove smoothly out of our parking lot.

* * * *

Dear Bridget. I watched her as she sprayed dusting compound on the window shelf and then gave the shelf a vigorous wiping. She had been here at the rectory for a long time, serving several of my predecessors. I tried to imagine her as a young woman who wrestled with some way to serve God. She'd told me once that as a teen she considered becoming a Nun but then decided that would be too constraining. She ended up falling in love but then fell out of love and, as she said, "I just decided to live my life," as if that explained everything.

I appreciate Bridget. She keeps my clothes tidy, sees to it that they get washed and that our floors get washed, too. Sometimes she will make me lunch if I'm home at the time. "Soup and a sandwich are no big deal," she says. And Bridget makes good, rich coffee.

I asked her about the Randall Dodge case.

"Oh, that poor man," she said. "Shot dead by someone and they don't know who did it."

"No, they don't."

"He was very rich. I read that in the papers. It was on TV. Someone shot him right in his own yard." She shook her head and murmured a soft cluck. "Poor man. Such a shame! And he left such a beautiful wife. Do you think they'll ever catch the person who killed him?"

"I don't think so. They may have some suspects but I don't think it will go anywhere."

Bridget turned to me and asked, "How do you know that?"

"Clergy confidentiality," I said. "I can't tell you how I know."

"Well," she said, "God knows for sure and eventually, when we all come to judgment, God will see that justice prevails."

"That's nice. So we wait under that promise, that God will deliver justice in the sweet bye and bye? I think we need some justice in the here and now. God's got some work to do!"

*   *   *   *

I was thinking about the media coverage, and as I stirred my instant coffee, I asked, "That was you?"

Derek nodded. For him, my instant coffee was bizarrely different than what he'd told me about the Sheriff's latte, with its steamed milk, served in a thin blue English bone china cup on a matching saucer that was oddly out of place in the Sheriff's utilitarian concrete block walled office. "Pretentious, moi?" the Sheriff had said. "It's OK; you're my secret weapon." Derek smiled as he told me the story. Sheriff Briggs served his coffee on a silver tray, the blue china cups and tray placed carefully on a gray steel side table next to his gray steel desk. I'd seen pictures of Sheriff Briggs, an imposing man with beef steak jowls, slicked back black hair greying at the temples, and a frame carrying a bit too much weight but adorned typically with a pinstriped dark woolen suit. He handled high profile cases like the Dodge case extremely well, especially with the news media.

I guess I'm a different story than Derek's boss, Sheriff Briggs. I'm tall and skinny, with a haircut that screams for a mother or wife's comb-through. Derek had told me about his boss, the Sheriff and his coffee. In contrast, I serve modest instant coffee in brown mugs to guests in this ornate jewel of an office, with its two richly colored stained glass windows, mostly reds and blues, and highly polished oak bookshelves and high-backed leather chairs arrayed around that round oak conference table across the room from my leather-topped desk.

"One shot through the right temple?"

"Yes," he said.

"Blood and gore all over the girl. Pretty ugly."

"Beats getting tossed over the bridge railing into the river. The ugly stuff can be washed off."

"But not the ugly stuff inside. She went through hell. That's not so easy to 'wash off.'"

Derek took a sip of the coffee. "I do my job," he said, "and counselors will do theirs."

I guess I nodded absently, considering where to take the conversation from here. "We talked about the morality of killing someone after you were called in for that guy down in New Ulm holding those group home kids captive," I ventured. "Do you still wrestle with that?"

"Not so much. I've done it so long that I guess I'm used to it. And as long as I can keep my body steady, I can keep doing it."

"But this stuff is different than being the Army's top sharpshooter. When we talked in the past, you told me about being the Brigade shooting champ. Fixed targets and mechanical moving targets are different than a human being."

"That's true," said Derek. "But the world is full of bad guys, if you haven't noticed. Someone has to deal with them and I guess I'm asked to be it. And that's after long negotiations have failed, when the other guys have done their best to talk someone down and to cool the situation. I'm the last resort."

He'd told me about the Sheriff's comment, "You're my secret weapon." "Yes," Derek said he thought, "Briggs, I do make you look good."

I don't know why this came out, but then I said," "What do you know about Augustine and his thoughts about a just war?"

"Augustine? You mean Saint Augustine?"

"The same."

"Wasn't he an early church Bishop?"

I nodded. "North Africa. The Bishop of Hippo."

"And?"

"Well, one thought of his—and this is somewhere between mid-300 and 450 or so C.E.—

is that using force is OK to enforce belief. So, if you stretch that to today, there should be no guilt about killing someone, even though one of the Commandments is 'Thou Shalt Not Murder'."

"But," he said, "what I do has nothing to do with belief in Christianity or any other belief system. It's just me, my skill, against some bad guy, an evil loose in the world."

"That's true, but it's still murder," I said. "That's a moral, ethical issue. And, yet, last week you were telling me about Charlene's behavior, as if it were worse."

"That's different."

I looked at Derek over the rim of my coffee mug and managed to keep my silence. It was a question, although he said nothing in reply.

Then: "When she decided to split, I went to counseling," he said. "So I understand the deal. That doesn't mean I like it. I understand that she grew up in a broke household, no money in a neighborhood full of people, families, who were not broke. I told you what she told me, that as a cop I'd always have an income ceiling, so why didn't I start my own security firm or something? What I provided just wasn't good enough. And, so, when he came along, Randy Dodge, Mr. Big Real Estate Developer, with his cream-colored Bentley and the big lake place he'd won in court by cheating the elderly widow, who just happened to be my aunt, Charlene went for it. Oh, I understand it. I understand it too well. It's not him; he's—he was— a jerk, a con, a bad man, but it was all about what he had and that meant what she could have, too. I understand all that! But it still sticks; it hurts deep down in my gut, even after this long."

I took another sip of my thin coffee. "Yes," I said, "Dodge was all that. Everyone knew it about him. And now the man is dead, shot in the head, right through the temple. Nice and clean. About as good as you can do. And you do have a motive. She told me she has what would seem to be a motive: he cheated flagrantly."

"I have no weapon at the house. Haven't had since Charlene and I split. I used to let her use my Winchester, the one I started with as a kid. Now, I keep my gear at the station and check it out when I'm called. Yes, I have a motive but there are others who have things against him, too. And I have to say, I don't feel bad about the guy dying. Lots of people hated his guts. Whoever got him got him as he was riding his big new mower along the lakeshore. The thing ran until he fell off the seat, they say."

"Blood and gore all over."

"That happens. You can wash off a lawn tractor."

"Have you talked with her?"

"Are you kidding? No."

Derek reminded me of his coffee with the Sheriff. "'You're my secret weapon,'" the man had said, "so you'd damned well better be clean! A scandal would be very bad, bad for me and. . . . " He'd raised his delicate coffee cup: "and bad for you."

"Not to worry," Derek had said. "I fish on my time off. I don't even do target practice. And as I said, there's no weapon in my house. I leave work at work. I leave it here."

Derek seemed to relish telling me that story.

He looked at me with a level gaze. "She has a motive, too," he said. "I gather you talked with her?"

I nodded. "I talked with her last week."

"She confessed, I'm sure."

"You know I can't disclose our conversation."

He smiled wryly, set his cup on the table, and rose to leave.

"Thank you, Padre. It's always a pleasure. But I've got to say, that even with a motive, and yes, I have one—I hated the guy— but it was not enough for me to kill him. And I'm an obvious suspect with the demonstrated skill to kill him with the skill it took to kill him in the way he was killed. Some people think I'm a likely suspect. I might be a suspect, but I'm not a fool. The station time clock has me working that day. I'm clear."

So, that's good. Both Charlene and Derek have solid alibis. It's unlikely they will be prosecuted. They should be safe. That makes me feel much better.

*   *   *   *

I'm not a detective of course, just a guy in over his head with some concerns about people I know and a passion for justice. That may make me look pretty foolish in the end. As I said, maybe I've read too many mystery novels or maybe I've spent too much time with British TV mystery stories that featured Anglican priests that always seemed able to figure out and solve the crimes that came their way. But, here I had two people I knew who both would have had good reasons to exact revenge from Randy Dodge. I wanted more assurance that they would be OK. How safe were they, really? Could they possibly be charged? But neither one of them helped me learn anything more than I'd read in the newspaper.

Maybe it was time to flesh out what I knew by consulting the man who wrote what I read in the newspaper.

There is truth in stereotypes, which is why we recognize them, and Jim Drake was the stereotypical newspaper reporter: hard drinking, chain smoking, coffee swilling, overweight and with flat feet. I bought the coffee for him to swill.

"Randall Dodge? Lots of people think he got what he deserved," he said. "Newly rich and flaunted it the way new money likes to do. Got rich in part by using non-union labor. When the union guys tried to cut his electric power cords or something like that, he hired armed guards to be on the construction sites day and night. And then he'd find a way to foist his bills onto his sub-contractors."

"If he did that," I asked, "Why did people work for him? Eventually, I'd think he'd run out of sub-contractors."

"Oh, they got paid some—eventually. But Dodge has such a big operation—he dwarfs everyone else—that there's always steady work." He gulped a mouthful of coffee. "Down time is what people in construction fear the most. That's why they tend to over-book, which is why you can't get a plumber or an electrician to come promptly when you need one."

"I don't deal much with that stuff," I said. "Bridget usually is around when we need help like that."

"Bridget? Is she still there?" he asked. "She's been there at the rectory forever! She was there when I was a kid. I thought she was dead."

"No, she's still with us. And she's doing fine. Dear Bridget, good old meticulous Bridget, who doesn't miss a thing and keeps me on track."

"Must be nice to have someone who cleans for you and who does your dishes. I end up doing all that myself."

"Drake, maybe you need a girlfriend," I said.

"For that, I'd need a miracle," he said as he drained the last of the coffee. "Maybe you could pray one up for me?" He looked at his watch and then leaned toward me along the counter. "Briggs has some suspects in this case; I'm sure of that," he said with emphasis. "Briggs has some very good people; they find out these things. He never misses. You saw I wrote a few weeks ago that they figure the shot that killed Dodge came from the lake, from someone on the water? You watch, Briggs'll go for Governor someday. I've seen these guys over the years and he's got *it.*" He straightened up. "Gotta go," he said as he padded toward the door. "There's a news briefing down at City Hall."

I added a dollar to the quarter tip he left on the counter.

*　　*　　*

Bridget was bustling around in another room and I just sat thinking about Randall Dodge. He'd been a pretty public figure. It seemed that everyone knew he was a slick dealer, not so much a con, but a man who would take advantage of people if he could. I'd heard about his womanizing and it bothered me that Charlene was victimized, if you can call it that, in that way. It certainly had to be something that shamed her. Did she deserve it? She'd left a good husband for what looked to her like greener grass with someone else. Was there true justice for Charlene, being left with plenty of money but probably without being able to know whom she could trust, both personally and financially? And where was the justice for a good man like Derek that she'd left?

And where was the justice for Derek's aunt, a little old lady who lost a court case brought by Dodge, who ended up taking possession of her lake property when she had no money for an appeal, destroyed her perfectly good house and built a mansion in its place? The new house was palatial, the kind that made people on the lake idle their boat engines as they drifted on the water, gawking and taking it all in. Where was the justice for Derek's aunt? She never saw it; I did her funeral and Derek said that being cheated out of what she'd known all her life broke her heart, which was why she died. Where was justice in that? Wasn't there something someone, anyone, could do to bring justice for these people? Why did that Baptist lawyer have to be right, that there was no justice to be found in this life?

It really bothered me, that lack of justice. Someone should do something!

Well, it looks like somebody did.

Dear Bridget was putting her arms into her coat as she got ready to leave for the day. "I did windows, mirrors and other some of the other glass things today," she said. "I cleaned your gun cabinet's glass, too. Oh, and the empty carrying case for that rifle you have at the repair shop, the one that's been there for awhile? I folded it neatly and I put it on the floor of the cabinet so that when you do get back that gun, the case is easy for you to find. And you'll be wanting to buy some ammunition; there are no more boxes in the cabinet."

"Thank you," I said. "You look after me well."

Dear, sweet Bridget, careful and meticulous as always. Yes, she does look after me well.

At Midnight's Stroke

By

Mark Hayes Peacock

We are sitting together in the living room while the nurses

turn Mother on her other side. My cousin Grace sips coffee

thoughtfully, while I munch cookies from a box and my younger

brother's widow Kayla chugs from her second high caffeine can of

soda. Some people think that one's loving family sits and sobs when

people are at their life's end. That's not so. There are tears, yes; but

after all the "remember when" recollections there is laughter over

shared family stories and plenty of "just talk", which is what we are

doing now.

I listen and learn.

"So she tells me she traveled to find her mother, met her and

spent most of the day with her," says Kayla. "But her mother didn't

seem all that interested in Laura. Her mother answered Laura's questions and all that but didn't ask about Laura or her family or her life. There just wasn't much there. It was very disappointing but Laura shrugs it off and says 'Life goes on' and for her I believe she means it."

"That had to be tough," says Grace.

"Well, sure! But Laura tells me that her adoptive mother and father always assured her that she was special, that they got to choose her instead of taking what randomly happened and that they loved her very much. So maybe that's why she can handle that disappointment with a bit of shrug."

"You know that I was adopted," says my cousin Grace. "I know my sister Linda didn't want to find her birth mother, but I did. And when I did, I found a bunch of people who looked like me, walked like me and who even had my same hairline."

"So how did you ever find your 'natural' family?" I ask.

"The agency, Phil. My parents said it was OK; it wouldn't hurt their feelings if I went exploring. It turns out that my actual parents were very young, not even halfway through high school. They weren't able to keep me, so I was put up for adoption. After that, they did get married and had three more children. My mother said she always wondered about how I turned out, what I looked like, how my life had gone."

The aides nod our way as they leave Mom's bedroom. We file in. Mom's bedroom is small; the women take the only two chairs; I stand. Mother's oxygen mask covers most of her face. She stares ceiling-ward. I can't tell if she might be in pain but in any case she is heavily medicated. Now there is no conversation, just the hiss of oxygen through the mask.

We sit in silence for some time. Finally, I take Mom's hand gently in mine. "It's OK, Mom; do what you need to do. Everyone here will be OK."

We sit in silence some more. Finally, Grace and Kayla take their leave, pledging to return tomorrow or the next day, depending on their kids' schedules.

I am left with Mom.

I look tenderly at my rock, the center of our home. She and my Dad have been so much for me, have done so much for me, have been the propulsion that launched me. I think people would say I'm very successful; I say I would not be that without them, who they are and were and how they raised me. Time and values; that's what they gave me. Positive reinforcement. Allowing me to fail in ways that would teach me but would not hurt me; that's what they did. My Dad giving hours and hours of playing catch and coaching my baseball team, teaching me how to handle a basketball so I could actually make free throws, throwing a football long so I'd really race to catch it, and both of them patiently coaching me through learning to drive so I've never gotten a ticket in all these years. I remember when we re-built my old Ford. Dad taught me to take my time, to be patient, to take pride in careful work.

I miss my Dad.

And Mom, always the encourager, drilling me patiently in things like my times tables, Latin declensions, chemistry valences and physics formulas. She put up with my inept spelling and tried to untangle my awkward English sentences. All that and cookies, fresh baked bread, squeezed oranges for juice no matter how many of my buddies "just happened" to be hanging out at our house. She took it all in stride, my Mom did. Maybe I have her temperament.

If I ever find the right person, which at my age still might be a possibility, I want to parent my kids the way my Mom and Dad parented me.

Mom is waving her hand, motioning in the direction of the chest beside her bed.

I know the delicate arch of that arm, the curve of that hand. It's immortalized in a photo I have on my den wall: my mother in one of her dance poses, taken, she told me, during rehearsals for one of the films in which she danced when she was barely out of her teens. She'd wanted to be a ballet dancer but there was no money in being part of a corps de ballet. There was money in film however, so she put her energy and talent into making movies.

She never had a speaking part. But she could move with grace and elegance. It made for good decoration.

As I said, though, Mom was far more to me than mere decoration.

I don't know what she is gesturing for. It's one of the last moves she makes before she dies.

Grace, Kayla and I reconvene in the office at the funeral home. I've managed to find the score from one of Mom's earliest films. We will get a pianist to play it. We agree on an obituary, the details Grace will flesh out and get to the funeral director. Yes, an open casket will be fine. OK, we will need about a dozen death certificates. No, Mom was not a Veteran. Hymns? We look at each other blankly. We didn't go to church much and about all I can remember from my childhood is "Jesus Loves Me", which may or may not be appropriate for a funeral. We will discuss it and decide. A soloist? Another person to pay; we tell the funeral director we will let him know.

I am surprised at the number of people who show up for Mom's funeral service. I didn't know she had that many friends. Some of them are people Kayla and Grace know and some are friends of mine. We end up with a soloist who does a nice rendition of "The Lord's Prayer". I can't handle reading the obituary so Grace does it. People say nice things to us as they file out to their cars to go to the cemetery.

It's windy on the hill overlooking the river valley and the pastor's garments move with the breeze. The service is brief and we throw handfuls of dirt on the casket that will be buried completely after we all leave. On my way down the hill I see two men in a truck in a cul-de-sac waiting to deploy their shovels.

We drive back to the church and the dining room is warm so we can thaw out. We eat the usual funeral fare: sandwiches, some cheese, Jello of various colors, and cookies for dessert. People are telling stories of my mother and I learn some things I didn't know. A few old women try to embarrass me by sharing what they remember of me when I was a small child. Still, I'm grateful they took the time to come to honor my mother.

During the next few days Grace and Kayla go through Mom's things. The clothing will go to Goodwill, costume jewelry to the high school drama department and the kitchen ware and dishes will be offered to children in the process of setting up their new households. We will offer Mom's furniture to the children, too.

Kayla and Grace leave and I am alone. I sit on the edge of Mom's bed, shorn of sheets and blankets. This is the bed in which I saw her last. I open the top drawer of Mom's bedside chest, the one she was gesturing toward with the grace of a young woman that she still retained decades later.

Under some pantyhose I see the envelope: "For Philip" it reads. I open the envelope and find a letter. It is written in Mom's precise hand, an old-fashioned script, cursive writing with well formed vowels and gentle tails on letters that should have them.

I read: *"My dearest Philip, Jerome, your Dad. was a*

wonderful Dad, as good as a father to you and devoted and

loyal to me. You are I were so fortunate to have

had him in our lives. While he was your Dad, he was not

your natural father. Philip, your actual father is Eldon

Grundhofer, who directed my last film. He lives in the big

white house on the corner of Lake Hollywood Drive and

Valley View Trail, the one with the round staircase that looks

like a turret, the one we used to drive by on our way to see

our friends, the Millers. Jerome knew about Eldon but he

didn't care; he cared about you and about me. For him—and

for me—the past was the past. I commend that to you, too.

It's enough for you to know but, more importantly, in the

light of that to appreciate Jerome, who had the courage to

take on both you and me and commit to us.

"Philip, I am sorry to tell you this by way of a letter, but I

just couldn't bring myself to do it face-to-face. There would

be too many questions and I'd have no good answers. Also,

there was no need for anyone else to know. This is for you and it's for you because I think it's only right that you do

know. Love, Mom"

I sit. I don't know what I feel. Fortunately, no one else is with me; I'd have no idea what to say. I put the letter back in its envelope and I notice my hands are shaking.

Mom is right; I couldn't have had a better Dad than Jerome. I think of him too often. Am I who I am because of Jerome's influence, because of how he raised me? Or am I who I am because of the genetics of someone else, a famous movie director with a couple of Oscars to his credit? I think of the truth of "the casting couch" and guess that was what it was about: my mother, young, talented and ambitious, and an older man with power and influence who could help that talent advance. Or at least that probably was the promise. And then I came along and the promise of talent, youth, and ambition went unfulfilled.

I help Grace's children move furniture and furnishings to their new places. It's wearing: I help one of them haul heavy things up three flights of stairs to his lofty apartment. I'm glad to do this just once. When they are older they will be able to afford to hire professional movers or somehow shanghai friends to help.

I push from below as we heft a sofa up flights of stairs. As I heave and shove, I think of the casting couch, so legendary and so true and so traditional. And I think about Eldon Grundhofer, the master of the casting couch. I've seen pictures of him, of course, just as any of the famous people who've had their pictures published in the media, especially when they've won an award or received some other recognition. The media showed him in a tuxedo when he accepted his awards. When shooting films on the set and on location he was famed for wearing high riding boots or safari boots. He affected a riding crop that he used to direct actors moving from one shot to another. Did Mom somehow focus my attention on him subtly enough so I never knew or was I aware of Grundhofer just because of his reputation? I'd never know. What I did know was public and probably not much more than any movie fan would know.

It would have had to be an OLD movie fan at that.

And so I find myself ascending the stone stairs of the imposing white house with the turret on the corner of Lake Hollywood Drive and Valley View Trail. Untamed green ivy creeps across the gray stones bordering the steps. The front door is weathered wood, heavy and once dark stained but now bleached by many southern California suns. There is a large corroded brass knocker and no doorbell. I use the knocker and it echoes inside the door and seems to broadcast itself down to the neighboring homes.

I wait. There is silence. Nothing. What am I doing here? What on earth do I think I'm doing anyway? Will he answer the door? What will I say? Will I be received like Kayla's friend Laura or will I be welcomed warmly like Grace's natural father and mother welcomed her?

I hear the sound of a lock turning and the door cracks open. Grundhofer stands there, blinking into the sunlight, looking far older than the newspaper and magazine pictures of him in a tuxedo accepting his award from the Academy.

"Yes?" His is a deep voice, an obviously trained voice, that of an actor turned director, which is how people become directors.

"My name is Philip Yanley," I blurt out. My words tumble out in a rush. "My mother was Elaine Grant. You directed her in 'At Midnight's Stroke'. I believe I'm your son."

He looks at me with what I think is pity and perhaps sadness. He stands silent for moments. I have the grace to wait. My hairline and his are the same; he has that same widow's peak. I have the same nose and the same furrow between my eyes. Yes, there is a resemblance. Am I looking at myself forty or fifty years from now? Does he see himself as younger again? His silence continues and so does mine. Will he invite me in? Will he embrace me, be glad to meet me?

"I'm afraid your belief is wrong," he says finally in that deep, slightly affected voice. "I've never had children and I don't remember any Elaine Grant."

"She was a dancer. Tall, blonde, graceful. There were other films but you did *At Midnight's Stroke* together."

He listens, cocking his head slightly but showing no sign of recognition. Finally, he says "I did *At Midnight's Stroke* and there were dancers but I don't remember anyone like the person you describe. I never knew any. . . ?"

"Elaine Grant."

"Any Elaine Grant. I'm sorry to disappoint you, son. I hope you do find the person you are looking for. And I do wish you well."

And, gently, he closes the door.

I don't know what I was expecting. I kick myself for being such a fool. Suddenly, I find myself in tears, perhaps for what might have been but thankful for Jerome and Mom. How different my life would have been if I'd been raised by Eldon Grundhofer.

I retrace my way down the gray stone steps to my car and soon find myself driving through the iron gates of the cemetery where Mom rests. Her grave is up this Avenue and up the hill. I park next to a spreading California oak tree. Her marker is ten steps to the left of the tree and I find it. I am crying again, perhaps for her hopes and dreams and perhaps for my feelings of guilt for having spoiled them.

I have Mom's letter in my jacket pocket. I take it out, consider her careful handwriting on the envelope, and then tear it into small bits and scatter them across her grave.

A light breeze wafts them all over the grass, bits and pieces of someone's life, someone's story blowing away.

Lost Wax

By

Mark Hayes Peacock

The small red runabout spun wide circles around the solitary swimmer. Circle after circle brought the boat closer and closer to her, with its sharp banking shooting a cascading spray of sparkling, glittering, shimmering sunlight-caught liquid diamonds raining over her as rippling tides from the circling boat's wake repeatedly trumped the fine shower, with both the spray and wake drenching her as she treaded water.

He cut the engine and, coasting, let the boat drift more slowly toward her. It bounced and rolled with the churning wake set up by the circles he'd spun around her. With several strong strokes she was at the boat's side. He stood and offered two hands. Taking his hands, she put one foot on the boat's strake and with strong arms he hoisted her so her other foot could be planted on the boat's gunnel.

She pushed and both tumbled onto the back seat cushion, his face buried beneath an umbrella of dark wet hair as she planted her mouth firmly on his.

Freeing one side of his mouth, he managed to get out the words, "I did rings around you."

"So I noticed," she said.

With his free left hand he fumbled for the small black felt box on the console between the front seats.

"There are other rings," he said. "I have one."

"Later," she said. "It can wait." And she buried his face again beneath her profusion of wet dark hair.

*   *   *   *   *

It had to be several years later when she was watching him consider the next color to be splashed onto the large canvas spread at his feet on the floor. He stood, contemplating: would it be best to drop some green or would red be better, especially in that upper right hand corner?

"Hon," she offered, "I think we need to talk about this a little." She handed him a mug of black coffee. He broke concentration and focused on her.

"We need to think about the future. There's a lot of time and work that goes into one of these," she said, motioning to the spattered canvas.

"True."

"And when you finish painting you have to cut it up and frame each piece and then we need to find some way to sell it."

He nodded and took a small sip of coffee.

"The real problem is that Pollock is already there. He has the media, he has the gallery, he has the marketing, he has the notoriety and he has all that already. The world doesn't need two Pollocks; he's already done what you are doing."

After a long pause he said, "And?"

"And it would be easier of you could create something that could be done once and repeated in a way that you wouldn't have to work so hard."

"Prints?"

"That's one solution. But I think people want something exclusive, or at least something that feels exclusive to them. Yes, prints are limited editions and if you're famous people will pay for having a number with your name attached. But you need to be famous first for prints to pay. At least that's what I think.

"Besides, a print lives on someone's wall. What if you could do something that would be more personal? *'Aristotle Contemplating A Bust Of Homer'* comes to mind; I don't recall anyone depicted someone contemplating a painting."

Ruminating, he said, *"A Bust Of Homer.* A statue?"

"Lost wax. Bronze casting. Create it once and it can be repeated many times. People can carry a small sculpture, move it, engage with it. You can hold it. It's tactile, a lot more physical than just being able to look at something."

He took another sip of coffee and walked slowly around the paint-spattered canvas on the floor. He stood, considering, deep in thought. She put her hand on his shoulder.

"The future, Jeff. We're running out of time to have a family. I can't be our sole support. You need to have a break-through. Maybe a change will do that."

"A casting of what? I have no idea of what to do or how to do it."

"You could learn the 'how' pretty quickly, I think. The 'what' is the question. Maybe something symbolic, something people can identify with."

"American eagle?"

"Probably overdone. But, yes, something American."

"An Indian."

"Too specific," she said. "We'd be sure to insult someone. Which tribe gets left out?"

They both stood silently for some time. Finally, she said, "The Great Plains are pure America but what impact is there in a casting of waving grain?"

"Wild horses," he responded.

"Bison!" she said.

And bison it was.

*   *   *   *   *   *

He did learn the craft of casting a bison in bronze, sculpting it first in clay, then transferring it to a plaster mold and then again and again to make wax or rubber duplicates of his original. He learned how to pack sand around his plaster molds, making sure channels were in the proper place so the molten metal could flow evenly to all the parts he designed for it and the molten wax would flow out: "lost". He found a used kiln that could heat his bronze to the 1,000 degrees it needed in order to pour smoothly. He learned how to crack open his plaster molds without damaging the finished sculpture. He found his own way to burnish the result and discovered which acid would give his pieces the patina he wanted. She hunted up a reliable source of red oak on which he mounted each bison. Trial and again he worked to cast so there would be no pits in the finished work.

He traveled to a farm in Minnesota that raised buffalo; he took pictures, he studied the way they moved, he saw how the wind ruffled the animals' hair. He watched them graze in the deep grass that rose to their bellies, just as it must have grown hundreds of years before on the Plains. He returned in the Winter and saw how the snow coated their backs and matted down their hair. He heard their snorting and saw them shuffle when they sensed he'd come too close. He wanted to get it right.

She delivered the first several castings to galleries she'd contacted in Iowa, South Dakota, Nebraska and Kansas. A month later she brought them several more. The next month saw a return trip. Sometimes, all the bison she'd brought the first time were gone, sold, and there was a check waiting. More often, at first, she simply had brought a few more for the shelf. Once in awhile she ended up taking home bison that had not sold in months. It was a matter of repetition, trying to nudge shop owners to move Jeff's bison closer to the front for better visibility and a better chance to sell. Later, on one hip she balanced the box of bronze bison she brought into the store by their first baby in a sling on the other hip.

One day she brought him coffee as he worked sculpting in the drafty garage they'd rented.

"Good news!" she declared as she handed him his mug.

He took a stool and waited.

"Remember that kid at the University, the one I told you was in film school? The one we met at the folk fest a couple of months ago?"

He nodded.

"His graduation thesis assignment is a documentary. I suggested you and what you do. He and a crew will be here next Tuesday."

He put down his coffee mug, picked her up, swung her around, and kissed her hard.

"What would I ever do without you?" he said.

"Yes, what would you do?"

"I need to clean up this place," he said. "There's really no room for cameras and lights. There's barely room for me and hardly any electricity."

"That's their problem, not ours. They'll find a way. You might want to think about a different shirt, though."

*　　*　　*　　*　　*　　*　　*

They watched the night the documentary was in the running for an award. The broadcast showed clips from each film and the University's clip showed Jeff concentrating as he sculpted and then as he opened a mold after a pour and cooling. The film didn't win but its broadcast resulted in several media interviews. "I'll do my best not to stammer," he'd told her. "I'm not used to this stuff."

She shrugged. "Get used to it," she said.

*   *   *   *   *   *   *

She had been thinking about the results of Jeff's public exposure. She caught his attention at breakfast one day before the children were awake.

"I've been thinking," she said.

"Why am I not surprised?" he said.

"Your image needs adjusting."

"Adjusting?"

"Adjusting. Bison are associated in the public mind with the Great Plains, with the prairie. And here you are, living in the big city. The garage costs us a fortune every month and I agree with you that it's way too small. We've talked about not wanting to raise our children in the city. Maybe you need to be in a place that matches what you do. Maybe there needs to be some congruity between place and product, if you know what I mean."

"I'm not sure I do."

"We need to get out of the city. You need to be in some small town somewhere, somewhere in or near the Great Plains. Your renewal from the routine will come from becoming rooted in the place where buffalo herds once roamed. It will be in the air, almost like their ghosts; you'll almost smell it! And maybe there will come something else, another thing like your bison. People may well want more from you than just one of your buffalo on their shelf. You have a following now and maybe you owe them something."

*   *   *   *   *   *

They brought the small red runabout with them when they moved to Brookings, South Dakota. There, on the edge of the vast prairie where buffalo once roamed by the hundreds of thousands, in a large Queen Anne they raised their family. Jeff enjoyed a big heated garage in which to work. He hired a local college student to help with the finishing of each sculpted piece. Jeff's bison became the symbol for The American Plains Preservation Fund, which bought hundreds of them each year as rewards to contributors above a certain giving level. The Fund asked Jeff to speak at several fundraisers and soon enough she saw to it that his work was brought to the attention of most of the major national land and wildlife conservation associations. She saw to it that the children were not allowed to interrupt their father when he was at work in the garage.

No more traveling by car or by van to galleries and shops to stock bronze sculptures; she hired two older women to help pack and ship them. In between making school lunches, shepherding homework and tucking children into bed, she somehow found time to tend to the cluttered desk with its invoices, correspondence and phone calls.

"What would I ever do without you?" he'd say.

"Yes, what would you do?" she would respond.

*　　*　　*　　*　　*　　*　　*

"I've got you booked to give a speech in November at the Lost America Coalition convention in Atlanta," she announced one day.

"A speech? I can't give a speech to them; they're huge; the place probably will have a thousand people. I don't think I can do it!"

"I'll help you," she said. "Just because you've never done it before a big crowd doesn't mean you can't give a good speech. Besides, you taught yourself how to cast buffalo in bronze; some practice and you can do a speech."

"I don't know what on earth I could say," he said.

"We'll figure it out. I said I'd help you."

He didn't look happy.

"Why don't you talk about why you think bison are so important? They almost went extinct, almost eradicated by humans. We may not be shooting all sorts of other species, but we certainly are killing them. We destroy their habitat. We poison them because we want to control turf that's long been theirs. Sheep farmers want to eliminate all wolves; chicken farmers want to get rid of coyotes and foxes. Bears interfere with people out camping. We try to regulate the deer population by creating official hunting seasons. Same for fish. There's lots to talk about."

"I know so little about all that. I'm an artist, not a zealot."

"Jeffrey Saltin, for the exposure this talk can give you, you can become a zealot! And I said I'd help you."

He gave the speech. It went well, just as she said it would.

*   *   *   *   *   *   *

She cornered him in his studio one afternoon just before quitting time. "I think you need a top-notch brochure," she said. "It's long overdue. I've booked a great photographer—two actually, one to do tabletops of the bison and the other to do a really great portrait of you."

He shook his head but she persisted.

"It's marketing, Jeffrey. Everyone does it. We should have done it years ago. You need an updated picture anyway. Maybe something brooding or something where you are focused on sculpting but your face is in full focus. The buffalo will get their own space, probably the cover. It has to be a five color cover, a rich bronze, to show just how good your work is. And, besides, I'd like to see a picture of my good looking guy framed and hung, maybe above the living room fireplace."

Protesting got him nowhere. They did the brochure. It came out well. She rearranged the family portraits in the living room so his craggy face took the central place.

"I've arranged a retrospective for you," she announced one afternoon. "It's at the County Museum of Art in Minneapolis. That's pretty close by. The art school across the street will be having a pour the same day; it will be a big deal for the students for you to show up."

"How many bison do they think they can display?" he asked.

"You have all your sketches. We still have some of your early canvases. And the bison are not all the same: some have raised heads, some are snorting or pawing the ground, some are running, some are eating. Besides that, they are all different sizes."

"I never did get around to casting much else, just bison. Are you sure about this?"

"After all these years, don't you trust me?"

He grinned. "What would I ever do without you?" he asked.

"Yes," she said. "What would you do?"

*　　*　　*　　*　　*　　*

It began with a stomach ache that didn't go away. Anti-acids didn't help. She felt increasingly weak and began to spend time in the afternoons on the living room couch. The evening meals became simpler, often just a frozen pizza in the oven. Jeffrey quit work in the garage around mid-afternoon and came to sit in the overstuffed wing chair next to the sofa where she lay. At her request, the older boy took over mowing the lawn. The eldest daughter volunteered to do the dishes. After some weeks of her incapacity, even the younger children made their beds before heading off to school.

Eventually, the cancer diagnosis made things official. She did the customary medical protocols that gave good results for some-- but not for her.

He held her hand softly late one afternoon as the Fall sun cast its weak rays into the living room. He felt the rings he'd given her those many years ago, the one on the boat and the other he slipped onto her finger as he repeated his vows to her in the echoing vaulted church space.

"What will I ever do without you?" he said.

"You'll do," she said softly. "You've always learned how."

He gazed at length at her wan face. "You created me," he said at last.

"No. You were always there. I knew you could do it all. And you can do it still."

There was no energy left for further conversation so he just sat and thought while she slept.

*   *   *   *   *   *   *

His children took part in the service. The older boy began to read from notes he'd written about his mother, collapsed into sobbing and gave his notes to his sister to finish reading. "Mother was our rock," she read. Recovering, the boy joined his sister to chorus together: "Tough? No kidding!" There was laughter from the assembled mourners. They'd come from near and a few people from afar. The local paper had a reporter stationed at the back of the church; this was Mrs. Jeffrey Saltin, after all, the wife of the famous sculptor. Years later major news outlets like TIME Magazine would note his passing, but the major media would not be mentioning hers. Instead, her passing was of note to the parents who sat with her in the bleachers at school games, to the fellow choir members who'd been privileged to hear her clear soprano, to the Chamber of Commerce members who'd experienced the muscle she could put behind an event or community charity drive, and to the neighbors who laid claim to knowing Jeffrey Saltin personally and who could testify that he was a real down-to-earth guy who would greet them on the street and who could be seen occasionally with his wife walking their Dalmatian dog. They were nice people, they'd say, real down-to-earth, plain folk.

The pastor took a stab at a fitting memorial sermon-and missed. Jeffrey wasn't really listening. He put his arms around the two children on either side of him. He knew, somehow, they would do very well. They were like their mother, strong determined and creative. About himself, he was not so sure. Despairing, he thought:

Yes, what will I do without her? She did make me, really she did.

Without her, what am I? Not much, next to nothing, just like the wax

that's lost in my sculpting. Today my bison live in protected areas;

otherwise, they wouldn't have survived. Maybe she was my personal

protected area; I didn't just survive; because of her I thrived.

Sometimes in the years after her passing he would take the small red runabout to a State park about 20 minutes north of town. They had kept the boat for sentimental reasons. If you were watching, you might wonder about the solitary figure that put his speeding craft hard down into tight and ever-smaller circles. Round and round he'd go at full throttle, sending up a spectacular spray trail and then he would cut the engine and simply drift in continuous circles, the small red boat bouncing in its own wake. He would let the boat glide slowly to a halt. And then he would just sit there. At sunset, he would bring the red runabout to the launching ramp, load it on its trailer, and head home by himself.

If you didn't know who it was, you might wonder about him and what he might be up to, carving tight circles in a speeding small red boat. And if you did recognize Jeffrey Saltin, you afforded him the privacy he seemed to need. After all, real down-to-earth plain

folk don't intrude.

Snow Job and the Four Dwarfs

Another Mangled Fairy Tale

by

Mark Hayes Peacock

Three of the seven dwarfs had decided to seek greener pastures. The first dwarf, who was broad-minded and never condescended nor looked down on anyone, became a Peace Corps Volunteer working with Pygmies in Gabon, Central Africa. Things really began to look up for the second dwarf when he became an assistant manager with a National Basketball Association team. The third dwarf enlisted in the military and found duty in Guantanamo reading poetry for four hours daily to an impeached former President of the United States.

That left four dwarfs, who were quite happy around a card table playing everything from poker to Old Maid. Where seven dwarfs would make things too cozy, just four dwarfs almost filled a booth at the local coffee shop where they would gather with other geezers to complain and declaim about how the world was going to hell in a hand basket.

Today, however, the topic was the local prince, who'd been off in the woods using his silver sword to hack his way through acres of brambles, vines and thickets.

"Reminds me of the little kid who was digging through a large pile of horse manure," said the first dwarf. "He figured that with all that horse dung there had to be a pony in there somewhere!"

But it wasn't a pony the young prince sought. He figured that with so much growth to hack through there had to be a princess at the end of his quest. *And when I find her,* he thought, *the first thing I'll do is to take up this mess with the Forestry Service and the Bureau of Land Management. It's a gigantic fire hazard; the whole thing could erupt in a holocaust and cause all sorts of damage! I'll talk with them as soon as the government ends its shutdown and there's someone's around I can talk with.*

And so the prince hacked away, swinging his silver sword right and left, stopping to rest occasionally and looking back to see how far he had come. It was slow going.

At last his sword broke through the undergrowth and he found himself in a clearing. There was a decrepit hut in the clearing with moss on its roof shingles, spider webs hanging from its soffits, windows in need of caulk, and a bucket of water by the door for the animals that had been watching the prince's slow progress through the forest's thickets.

And there in the clearing on her back with her eyes closed, lying on a bed of willow branches padded with moss, lay the most gorgeous creature the prince had ever seen. She wore a sky blue gown with a plunging neckline and had a gold belt around an impossibly narrow waist. Her feet boasted black patent leather slippers. Her dark hair framed a heart-shaped face of ivory skin and her eyelashes were so long that when they were batted they could have created a draft in even a very large room. Her ruby lips invited discovery.

The prince sheathed his sword and circled the beautiful maiden. He figured she had to be a princess; no one else could have boasted the physical qualities he saw in front of him. His quest had not been in vain.

But now what? He touched her shoulder. No response. His princess still slept. Gently, he shook her shoulder. Still, no response. *If I tickle her feet?* he thought but wiggled her foot instead. No response. The princess still slept. "Hello?" he said. Nothing. "Hello!" he said in a louder voice. Nothing.

Then it dawned on him: what was needed was a kiss, just like in the fairy tales his mother had read to him when he was a child. *This will be easy,* he thought as he bent over her somnolent form. But as he lowered his face to hers the hilt of his sword jabbed him in the ribs.

"Damn, I forgot!" he said aloud. "These days you have to ask permission."

But how to ask when the recipient of a future kiss was so fast asleep that she couldn't assent? Nothing the prince had done so far had caused the princess even to stir. Casting around him, the prince thought there might be something that would make a very loud noise so his princess would awake. He found nothing.

But then he saw the water bucket. He strode to the shack door, picked up the wildlife's water bucket and brought it to the princess' bedside. He dumped the entire bucket full on her head.

In addition to waking up the sleeping princess, the water swept her eyelashes to the ground. Pale skin dribbled into her dark hair and down onto the bed. Those ruby lips remained but now against her skin the botox job was obvious.

"Who are you and what the hell do you think you're doing?" she demanded.

"I was just trying to wake you up," he responded, more than a bit startled.

"You did a great job!" she said. "And what was your need to wake me up, may I ask?"

"Well, that's how it's supposed to turn out," he said. "Besides, I worked hard for weeks just to get here and to find you!"

Warily, she eyed the prince. "Are you delivering a subpoena?" she asked.

"A what?"

"A subpoena? Are you one of those process servers—or whatever they call you?"

The prince laughed. "No," he said with great charm. "I am a prince with a kingdom to inherit and I'm in need of a princess to go with it. And now I've found you."

"What a con," she said. "Kingdoms. Princes. Princesses. All those are relics of the past. I don't believe a word of it!"

"But it's true! I really am a prince. Look, I'll prove it: here's my singing sword."

He took his sword from its scabbard and handed it to her.

"It's dull," she said.

"Of course it's dull; I've been hacking away with it for weeks now just to get to you, so of course it's dull."

"Show me an I.D."

The prince looked perplexed. Tunics and tights have no pockets and princes have no wallets. They always borrow what they need from their servants, footmen or butlers.

He took back his sword. "I can't show you an I.D.," he said. "I don't need one. Everyone in the kingdom knows me so all I have to do is wave back."

She gave the prince a once up and down. He did look like he could be a prince. "Let's go in the house," she said. "I need a mirror."

"Why don't we go to your castle?" he proposed.

"There is no castle. This is my refuge, my getaway."

Flummoxed, the prince trailed her into the miserable hut.

She found a mirror and stood aghast. "Look what you've done!" she said.

The prince didn't know what to say. "I need to do some repair work!" declared his princess and she disappeared through a heavy and creaking wooden door.

"You're new around here?" croaked a voice from the shadows on the far side of the room. In the dim light the prince could make out a small form. As it began to move into the light the prince saw an old crone that continued to speak.

"She's right about no castle," said the crone. "She's no princess, either. But this is her getaway, just as she said. Here, she can be treated as if she were a princess. For that matter—and as a young man it's good for you to know this—every woman at heart wants to be treated like a princess."

"So this is like some sort of spa?"

"You could say that. Here, she gets the royal treatment: massage, sunbathing, a chance to get out of those pantsuits and to dress up, eat organic food and to escape from fluorescent lighting and a corner office.

"She didn't have a chance to tell you. She's the owner and CEO of the major gold mining company in this area. Her days are spent meeting with legislators and regulators and environmental groups and even with the miners. Lots of pressure; that's why she takes a break here."

"And you?"

The crone shrugged. "I'm just here." Then, changing the subject back to the not-princess, she continued, "As I said, she deals with a lot."

"And they're all ungrateful!" declared the princess, who returned to the room after managing to re-install her false eyelashes and re-make her face. "A bunch of ignoramuses, especially those environmentalists. As for the miners, they're a bunch of ingrates! I talk until I'm blue in the face about the benefits I bring to everyone: jobs! I'll say it again: jobs! For every dollar those lousy miners earn, seven more are generated into the local economy. And, someday, we will go back to the gold standard and everyone around here will be rich. Rich, I say, rich!"

"Who would object to that?" asked the prince.

"Yes, who? Those regulators, politicians and environmentalists don't understand how much better my planned approach will be than the way gold has been mined before. No more tunneling! To do that economically you need narrow tunnels. For narrow tunnels, you need dwarfs. These days, dwarfs are hard to find; they've been a shrinking commodity since 'The Wizard of Oz'!

"So my plan is to change the entire industry of gold mining. Instead of tunneling into the mountain, I'll just level it. And that's Biblical: the prophet Isaiah said 'Every valley shall be filled, and every mountain and hill shall be made low', so even the conservative evangelicals around here ought to be happy about my plan. But no; it has to be a big fight! All I'm asking for are fewer regulations, some tax relief, and to be exempt from the fund to treat gold lung disease. In return, I'll bring jobs, jobs, jobs to this region! Did you hear me? I said JOBS! And if you're really a prince, you ought to have some influence around here."

The prince didn't know quite what to say. Jobs wasn't something he could relate to. "So no more dwarfs?" he asked.

"Ingrates! They all quit and went to town. Without them and with small tunnels, I really need to make those changes I was talking about."

She turned on her heel and left through the same large door, tossing over her shoulder as she went a request for perfumed water whenever the crone could bring it.

"Nap time," observed the crone. She took an apple from a bowl on the table and found a small sharp knife. Carefully, she sliced the apple into equal pieces and put several of them on a plate in a tray intended for the princess. Offering a slice to the prince, she said, "They're organic. Golden Delicious. Try one."

Back in the village the geezers nursed the last of the morning's coffee and watched the four dwarfs enter their limousine as their chauffer held the door open for them. They fit easily into a single back seat.

"They can't be called dwarfs anymore; it's not politically correct," observed the third geezer, a retired professor. "They're 'VC's'."

"VC's? Viet Cong?"

"No, VC's: 'Vertically Challenged'."

"Must be nice," said the first geezer. "Gold lung disease. They cough, up comes some gold, they put it in a hankie, take it to the assayer and get cash in return."

"That's how they fund their retirement," said the second geezer. "All because there's gold in them thar hills!"

"They earned it," said a third geezer. "Mining's hard work."

"Beats what you did all those years," said a fourth geezer. "University professor. Tenured, so you couldn't be fired. Got your grad students to do your research so you could write the papers and get all the credit and all those guest speaker fees. I don't mind seeing those little guys come out OK."

The third geezer turned bright red. He snatched the cardboard cylinder from the fourth geezer. "Gimmie those damned dice!" he said, as he tossed them and lost. "Black coffee for your black heart!" he said as he reached for his wallet.

The wallet-less prince thought the crone's apple was quite good and said so. Then, making conversation, he asked, "So, how long have you been an old crone?"

"Ever since I had a big change in my life," she replied. She peered at the prince over the tops of her glasses. "Young man, another thing for you to know is that inside every old woman is the girl she was when she was sixteen. Understand that and they'll all think you are a real prince of a guy!"

She sliced another apple, placed the slices on a plate and held the plate out to the prince. Suddenly realizing his hunger after all that time hacking away at the brambles and thickets, the prince reached for the plate she proffered and missed. The plate dropped to the floor and broke. Quickly, both crone and prince knelt to pick up the fallen apple slices and pieces of the broken dish. Face to face on hands and knees their eyes met. Drawn as if by some magnetic force their faces came closer together and with their kiss the crone instantly transformed into a beautiful young woman with natural long eyelashes, hazel eyes beneath them, smooth ivory skin and lips that invited a repeat meeting of their lips.

"I don't believe it!' said the prince. He stood, extended his hand and helped her to her feet. "What happened to you? How did you ever get that way? Did you have old crone's disease?"

" Sometime I'll tell you," she said with a smile. . "It's a bit like one of those old fairy tales and it has something to do with the

Golden Rule. You were being gallant, a gentleman, and so you see the result."

"Are you a real princess then, like in the fairy tales?" asked the prince.

"Only if you make it so," she said.

The prince grinned and said, "I think we could work that out."

About Mark Hayes Peacock

Mark published his first work, a poem, in the *Junior Journal*, a magazine for and by teenagers. Later, while in graduate school he wrote and edited a weekly publication for Los Angeles' *Town Hall*. His first national magazine piece appeared in 1971. That was followed by more than forty years of freelance articles, magazine cover articles and lead pieces, contributing editorships, and monthly columns in national, regional and local newspapers and magazines. He was the last regularly published Wisconsin freelance writer featured in the *St.Paul Pioneer Press.*

Mark is a semi-retired pastor married to retired mental health counselor Marina H. Peacock. They raised a brood of successful children and now live on Bone Lake, just outside of Luck, Wisconsin.

Other Story Collections by Mark Hayes Peacock

Paperbacks:

The First Gathering of The Break Time Stories

The Second Gathering of The Break Time Stories

Some Mangled Fairy Tales

EBooks

Four Break Time Stories

More Break Time Stories

Yet More Break Time Stories

Four More Break Time Stories

Yes, More Break Time Stories

Another Four Break Time Stories